*For Nick Cholis,*
*Nicholas P. Bear & Elly Roach*
*~A.M.*

*For Miles & Bruin*
*~J.M.*

LITTLE TIGER PRESS
1 The Coda Centre, 189 Munster Road, London SW6 6AW, UK
www.littletigerpress.com
This edition published 2002
Originally published in Great Britain 1999
ISBN 1 85430 883 1
1 3 5 7 9 10 8 6 4 2

# The CHRISTMAS Bear

ANNE MANGAN and JOANNE MOSS

It was nearly Christmas, and it was snowing. Inside the shop, among all the other toys, a little bear was delighted. He was a polar bear, and loved snow.

Now that it was Christmas he hoped that he would get a home at last. He had been waiting for a long time. He was sure that someone would spot him in the window, and want a bear to match the Christmas snow, but he was passed by every time.

"Someone must want me," thought the little bear gleefully, when he felt someone lift him from the window – until he heard her mutter, "That bear won't sell. He's taking up good window space."

The little bear was put on a high shelf inside the shop, to make room for a cute pink teddy. He sat there between a yellow monkey and a big doll.

"The longer you are in the shop the higher you go,"
whispered the monkey. "We're all forgotten now.
Children look on the lower shelves."
"Why wasn't I sold?" asked the little polar bear.

"Wrong shape and color," said the monkey. "You look rather like a teddy bear, but you're not one. I've not been sold because I'm too yellow."

"And I'm too expensive," said the big doll.

"Cheer up! We can see lots of things from here."

The shop looked very cheerful with all the Christmas decorations, but a shop wasn't like a home, thought the little bear. He began to feel quite dizzy.

"I know. I've just thought of something," said the monkey — and he wriggled off the shelf, right into a child's arms!

"You could do that," the doll told the little polar bear. "I'd be too afraid," he said. "I daren't either," said the doll. "I would break." So the big beautiful doll and the little polar bear sat side by side, and waited and hoped . . .

A week before Christmas a lady and a little boy
came into the shop to buy a present for his sister.
"Becky already has lots of dolls," he said.
"I want something different."
The little polar bear's heart lifted. He certainly
was different. The assistant reached up and
took him down off the high shelf.

"He looks like a mistake," said the lady rudely.
"People will think we got him cheap."
They chose a calculator instead.

The little bear felt his insides sagging.
It was awful to be a mistake.
He flopped right over, and
someone picked him up,
gave him a shake,
and set him back
in his place.

The next day a girl came into the shop. She wanted a pretty toy to sit in her room and look nice. She saw the doll on the high shelf. "Exactly what I've been looking for," she cried. The big doll was overjoyed. She didn't want to be hugged and loved as the little polar bear did. She just wanted to look pretty.

The little polar bear missed the big doll dreadfully. He sat on his high shelf all alone, while people came in and out of the shop in a last minute rush to buy their presents for Christmas.

He saw so many toys being sold, and he wanted a home more than ever. If only someone would choose him!

It seemed as though the little polar bear's wish was granted, for suddenly someone looked up at him and said, "What a jolly little bear. I'll have him for my youngest. It's her birthday today." The little polar bear was delighted. He didn't mind being bumped along in a bag, all the way to his new home.

"I've a lovely surprise for you!" the lady told her small girl. "Look!"
"Ugh!" said the child. "I don't want a silly bear. I wanted a racing car, you know I did." She threw the little bear across the room. Her mother picked him up again. "All right, darling. I'll change him for a car, shall I?"

The little polar bear was
bumped all the way back
to the shop, and put
back up on the high
shelf once more.

He felt worse than ever.

He had given up
all hope of ever
being wanted
and loved.

On Christmas Eve a man and a woman with cheerful faces came into the shop.

"We'd like to buy a Christmas present for our niece," said the woman.

"A doll?" asked the assistant.

"Well, I don't know if she likes dolls," said the man, "some do and some don't."

The man was so tall that he could see the high shelf easily. He noticed the little polar bear at once.

"How about this little fellow, Nicola?" said the man, taking down the little polar bear. "He's nice and soft. And snow-white like the North Pole."
"Yes, I think Elly will like him, Nicholas. Do let's buy him."

The little polar bear felt happy and afraid, all at the same time. "Suppose Elly doesn't like me?" he thought. "Suppose she thinks I'm a mistake? Suppose she wants a racing car instead?" He worried and worried as he was wrapped up in a Christmas parcel for the next day.

On Christmas morning, Uncle Nicholas and Aunt Nicola arrived at Elly's home. "We've an extra special present for you, Elly," said Uncle Nicholas. Elly felt the parcel. It was very soft, like something she wanted to hug.

Then she opened it. Elly looked at the little bear, and the little bear looked at Elly. "Do you like him?" asked Aunt Nicola.

Elly picked up the little bear and hugged him.
She buried her face in his soft fur.
"Oh yes," she cried. "He's the nicest present
I've ever had. I'll call him Nicky, after you both."
Elly took Nicky outside to let him see the snow.
Now the little polar bear had a home and a
name, and someone to give him lots and
lots of hugs. He was the happiest
little bear in the world!